WAFFLES THE CHICKEN IN THE KITCHEN

KEN AND ASHLEY MATTHEWS

To Liberty, the original Chicken in the Kitchen.

www.wafflesthechicken.com
email: info@wafflesthechicken.com
Rooster and Hen Publishing
Waffles the Chicken in the Kitchen
Copyright © 2020 by Ken Matthews
All rights reserved.
No portion of this book may be used or reproduced in any manner without written permission, except in the case
of brief quotes embodied in articles and reviews.
ISBN: 978-1-953352-00-2

Waffles the chicken woke bright and early, ready to eat.

There was no food in his dish.

The sun peeked over the hill.

Worms poked their heads out of the ground and the early birds rushed to get them.

Waffles walked across the field on his way to the farmer's house.

"Good morning, dog!"

"Good morning, cat!"

"Good morning, mouse! Sorry I can't play, but I'm much too busy today!"

Waffles did something new. He walked up the steps of the farmer's house and went inside.

He went into the kitchen, got a plate, and put it on the counter.

Now, maybe you have never seen a chicken before.

Chickens are quite small, and kitchen counters are quite tall. He made so much noise that he woke farmer Rachel.

Grocery
- Pickles
- Tuna
- Corn
- Bananas
- Penguins

She stood in her pajamas and watched him work.

First, he grabbed two slices of bread.

Then he grabbed some ham.

Next, a thick wedge of cheese.

Then lettuce, tomato, and a very large, very crunchy pickle.

He put it all together into a sandwich fit for a king.

What could it be?

Aha!

A glass of milk!

He turned and looked up at farmer
Rachel with a big smile.

"For me?" she asked.

Waffles the chicken nodded.

Waffles smiled and said, "I thought you might be hungry."

Farmer Rachel stopped smiling.

She sat Waffles on her lap and said, "Thank you for making me a sandwich. I will feed you because I love you, not because you made me something."

She gave him a hug and sent him on his way.

It read:

Thanks for reading!

If you love Waffles, there's plenty more! Join us at www.wafflesthechicken.com for FREE printable coloring pages and updates on new releases.

Don't forget to check out other books in the Waffles the Chicken series!

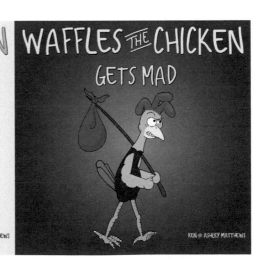